GPER

AUG   2018

Dear Parents:

Congratulations! Your child is taking the first steps on an exciting journey. The destination? Independent reading!

STEP INTO READING® will help your child get there. The program offers five steps to reading success. Each step includes fun stories and colorful art or photographs. In addition to original fiction and books with favorite characters, there are Step into Reading Non-Fiction Readers, Phonics Readers and Boxed Sets, Sticker Readers, and Comic Readers—a complete literacy program with something to interest every child.

Learning to Read, Step by Step!

Ready to Read   Preschool–Kindergarten
• big type and easy words • rhyme and rhythm • picture clues
For children who know the alphabet and are eager to begin reading.

Reading with Help   Preschool–Grade 1
• basic vocabulary • short sentences • simple stories
For children who recognize familiar words and sound out new words with help.

Reading on Your Own   Grades 1–3
• engaging characters • easy-to-follow plots • popular topics
For children who are ready to read on their own.

Reading Paragraphs   Grades 2–3
• challenging vocabulary • short paragraphs • exciting stories
For newly independent readers who read simple sentences with confidence.

Ready for Chapters   Grades 2–4
• chapters • longer paragraphs • full-color art
For children who want to take the plunge into chapter books but still like colorful pictures.

STEP INTO READING® is designed to give every child a successful reading experience. The grade levels are only guides; children will progress through the steps at their own speed, developing confidence in their reading.

Remember, a lifetime love of reading starts with a single step!

Step into Reading, Random House, and the Random House colophon are registered trademarks
of Penguin Random House LLC.

Visit us on the Web!
StepIntoReading.com
randomhousekids.com

Educators and librarians, for a variety of teaching tools, visit us at RHTeachersLibrarians.com

ISBN 978-0-7364-3519-2 (trade) — ISBN 978-0-7364-8232-5 (lib. bdg.)
ISBN 978-0-7364-3520-8 (ebook)

Printed in the United States of America   10 9 8 7 6 5 4 3 2 1

DISNEY·PIXAR

FINDING DORY

OCEAN OF COLOR

by Bill Scollon

illustrated by the Disney Storybook Art Team

Random House New York

Dory is a blue fish
who lives in the sea.

Marlin and Nemo
are orange fish.

Dory remembers
her mom and dad!

They are blue,
like Dory.

Dory swims
into the deep,
dark ocean.

She wants to find
her mom and dad.

Dory meets Hank.

He is red.

Bailey is a beluga whale.

He is white.

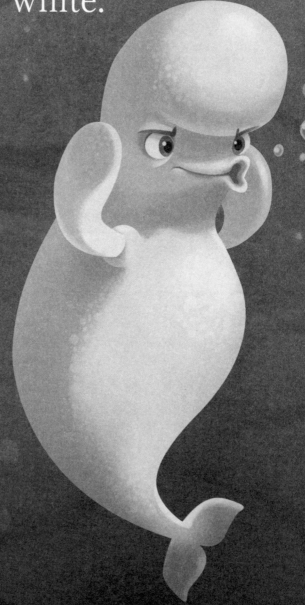

Destiny is a whale shark.

She has white spots.

The otter is brown.

He loves to cuddle.

Becky is a loon.

Her feathers are black,

blue, and white.

Dory sees a
purple sea urchin.

Dory finds many fish.
They are lots of colors.

Dory spies some
pink coral.

She is home!

Dory sees yellow fish.
She does not see
her mom and dad.

Dory swims through
the green kelp.

Dory sees two fish.

They are blue, like Dory.

Dory finds
her mom and dad!

Dory loves her colorful
family and friends!